Zed Storm has lived in Japan for the past five years and is a master of several martial arts. He has a wolfhound called Max, and in his spare time plays the guitar and competes in triathlons. He likes to read about history, space exploration and rare animals and he came up with the idea for Will Solvit while camping in a Siberian forest.

ATTENTION: ALL READERS!

Wherever you see something that looks like this, reach for your decoder! Holding it by the pink line, place the centre of your decoder over the lines. Rotate it very slowly, look closely and a picture will appear.

Mystery solved!

AND THE KNIGHTS OF REVENGE

DISCARDED

PaRragon

Bath New York Singapore Hong Kong Cologne Delhi Melbourne

Written by Zed Storm
Creative concept and words by E. Hawken
Check out the website at www.will-solvit.com

First edition published by Parragon in 2010

Parragon
Queen Street House
4 Queen Street
Bath BA1 1HE, UK

ISBN 978-1-4454-0458-5

Printed in China

Please retain this information for future reference.

CONTENTS

CHAPTER ONE
THE LONG ROAD TO ADVENTURE

"What happened to the blind skunk?" asked Zoe, as the school bus drove along the motorway. We were two hours in to the most brain-numbing journey EVER.

Dull

"I don't know," I shrugged. "What happened to the blind skunk?"

"He fell in love with a fart!" she giggled.

"Haha! Nice one, Zoe! My turn!" I laughed, as Mrs Jones turned around and glared at us from the front of the bus. "What's invisible and smells like carrots?"

"Dunno," said Zoe.

"Rabbit farts!" We both exploded with

laughter. Zoe's the only girl I know with the same awesome sense of humour as me.

"Here's another one..." I said, ignoring my school teacher storming down the bus aisle towards us. "How can you tell if a lady is wearing tights?"

"That's enough, Will Solvit!" screamed Mrs Jones in my ear. I looked up and she was standing next to me, hands on her hips and looking M.A.D. "The rest of the coach does not want to listen to your disgusting jokes," she said through gritted teeth. "I should have known better than to let you two sit together. Will, get up and move to the front of the coach – there's a free seat behind me."

Great – not only did I have to sit through the most boring coach journey of my life, I had to do it without anyone to talk to.

I followed Mrs Jones to the front of the coach, sat down and pulled my SurfM8 out of my bag. My SurfM8 is a really cool phone that has the internet and instant messenger on it.

I IM'd Zoe straight away – I knew she'd want to know the end of the joke.

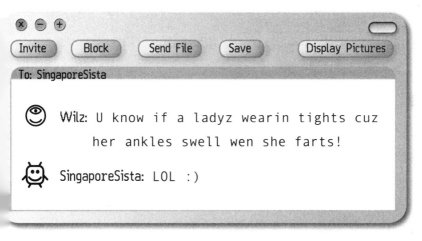

Zoe and I spent the rest of the bus journey IMing each other fart jokes. It turned into a competition – who could tell the grossest, funniest, rudest bum joke. I won, of course.

The coach rolled through miles and miles of countryside – it felt like we were heading into the middle of nowhere. Our whole class was being taken on a history trip to a mega-old castle. We were staying there for a couple of nights – everyone was pretty buzzed about being away from home. Not me though – I'm used to being away from home.

I'm an Adventurer, you see – everyone in my family is. Actually, I'm a Time Travelling Adventurer, to be precise. The only people that know I'm an Adventurer are my best friend Zoe, my Grandpa Monty (who I live with) and his driver, Stanley. It's my job to travel through time and solve mysteries. But I still haven't been able to solve the biggest mystery of all – where my parents have disappeared to.

To cut a very long story short, my parents went missing and I need to find them. The thing is, they could be anywhere in time. And the whole history of time is a pretty big place to try to look for people.

Finally, the castle was in sight. It was surrounded by hills and fields, and its tall grey turrets stuck out of the landscape like concrete mountains.

Everyone on the bus let out a loud cheer as we drove towards it.

The castle was surrounded by a wide moat. There was a large gate in the castle's battlements, and as we approached, the gate opened and a drawbridge lowered down for the coach to drive over. The castle courtyard was filled with a well-kept lawn that had a sign on it saying 'Keep Off the Grass'.

The coach pulled up by the castle entrance and everyone piled off. A flag flapping on the top of the castle caught my eye. The flag had a symbol on it that looked familiar – it looked like the amulet I wear around my neck. I've had my amulet since I discovered I was an Adventurer. It does some pretty cool tricks, like opening locks and helping me understand other languages. I peered hard at the flag, trying to get a better look, but it was getting dark outside and I couldn't really see.

Zoe and I met up as we collected our bags outside the bus.

"Mega-boring ride," Zoe said, rolling her eyes.

"Tell me about it," I replied. "Good job we had..." Something small, white and square caught my eye on the ground, and I forgot what I was saying.

"You seeing what I'm seeing?" Zoe said in a whisper, pointing towards the ground.

I nodded and headed straight for the white envelope – just as I suspected, it had my name on it. Letters arrive for me in weird places when an Adventure is about to begin. The letters give me clues that help me solve mysteries. Don't ask me who sends the letters though. I have no idea.

Carefully, so no one else saw, I ripped the envelope open and read the letter inside.

WHERE DO KNIGHTS GO TO GRAB A BITE TO
EAT?
AN ALL-KNIGHT DINER!

IT'S TIME FOR ANOTHER ADVENTURE, WILL.
AND IT'S FINALLY TIME TO HAVE SOME OF YOUR
QUESTIONS ANSWERED...

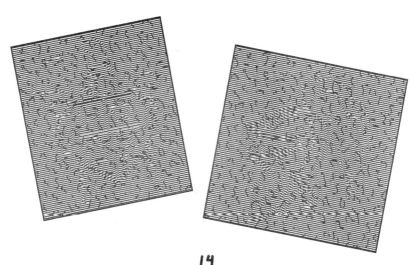

These are the top 10 questions I would like answers to:

1. Where are my mum and dad?
2. How did Mum and Dad get separated in time and space?
3. Why are bogies green?
4. Why did dinosaurs become extinct?
5. Is Grandpa Monty really as crazy as he seems?
6. Why are girls (apart from Zoe) so annoying?
7. How does my dad's invention Morph work?
8. What does alien Partek poo look like?

Spiky?

9.   How much longer until I find my parents?
10. Can a person survive on a diet of ear wax, bogies, the scum between toes and orange juice? *Yuk!*

Since the letter told me that some of my questions were finally going to be answered, I hoped that would include at least two of my top 10. Top of the list are the questions about Mum and Dad, but I'd settle for answers to the question about a bogie diet if I had to.

Avalon Castle (that's where my class was staying) is hundreds of years old. Apparently knights, lords and ladies used to live here, but now it's just used to teach school kids about history. If you ask me, the best way to learn about history isn't by studying books and going on school trips – it's by going back in time and seeing things for yourself.

"Follow me, class!" Mrs Jones instructed. She led us into the castle and down a stone corridor. The corridor was lined with large paintings of people in old-fashioned clothes.

"Don't you think this place is kind of spooky?" Zoe said, as we walked through the castle corridor. "I feel like I'm being watched. Maybe it's haunted?"

Trust a girl to be scared!

"There's no such thing as ghosts," I assured her. I was used to slightly spooky buildings. Solvit Hall, where I live with Grandpa Monty, has been in my family for generations – most people think it looks like a haunted house, but it doesn't scare me. And I've never seen a ghost there – yet.

Mrs Jones stopped walking when the castle

Woooooooooo

17

corridor split off in two directions. "Since the journey took so long," she yelled loudly, her voice echoing off the stone walls, "I think it's best if everyone goes straight to bed tonight and we start our lessons in the morning."

A loud groan came from us kids – no one wants their school teacher telling them when to go to bed!

"The girls' dormitory is to the left," Mrs Jones continued, "and the boys' is to the right."

"I'll IM you," Zoe said, as Mrs Jones ushered her and the other girls towards their dormitory.

I headed to the boys' dormitory. It was HUGE – I reckon it must have been a banqueting hall back in the olden days. The stone walls were decorated with frayed and faded tapestries, there were large suits of medieval armour up against the walls (very cool, by the way) and wooden beams were holding the ceiling up. No large, fancy beds though – just small beds in a row against the walls. I sat down on my bed and took out my SurfM8.

Wilz: Wanna go explorin afta lights out?

SingaporeSista: Dunno...

Wilz: Chicken!

SingaporeSista: Am not!

Wilz: Cluck cluck!

SingaporeSista: Fine

Wilz: Cool, meet me outside ur dorm in 20

As soon as the lights were off, I snuck out of the boys' dormitory. None of the other boys even bothered to get up and go exploring – BORING!

I knew the castle would be dark. Luckily I'd packed some of my dad's omnilumes (sticks that can turn night to day), so I put one in my pocket, in case I needed it to light the way. I met Zoe outside her dorm. She was wearing a dressing gown and slippers.

"Are you sure this is a good idea, Will?" she asked, pulling her dressing gown tightly around herself and shivering.

"Of course it is!" I said. "How many chances do we get to explore castles? None! So we need to do as much as possible. Besides, I've got another Adventure to go on, remember? There might be important clues here that I need to find." Zoe nodded her head.

So off we went.

It was freezing cold. We tiptoed over the castle's stone floors so no one could hear us. Moonlight crept through the large glass windows and lit up the winding corridors as we walked through them. The walls were lined with old pictures of knights fighting dragons, knights in chain mail, kings with fur cloaks and jewelled crowns and people fighting with swords. I could have sworn the eyes of the people in the pictures were following us. Zoe was right: being in the castle felt like someone was watching you.

The more we walked around, the more creeped out I became – but I'd never admit that to Zoe! The wind outside was rattling the castle windows

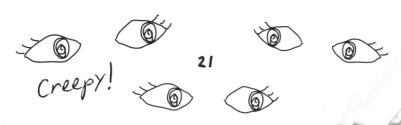

Creepy!

21

and making an eerie howling sound. It sounded like voices were being carried on the wind...

I tried to snap myself out of any chicken-like fear and focus on what I had to do. I was on the lookout for another letter, or something that might give me a clue to my next Adventure.

The corridor we were walking down led to a narrow staircase that wound upwards. It was pitch black on the staircase – no moonlight to help guide the way. I took an omnilume from my pocket, snapped it so it lit the way and started to climb. The steps were steep and narrow and worn down in the middle from years of being trodden on. There were so many steps to climb that my legs were aching by the time we got to the top.

There was a tiny door at the top of the staircase, but there was no handle and no lock.

Next to the door was a small portrait of an elderly man with long white hair. Underneath the picture was the man's name, Lord Avalon.

"Do you think Lord Avalon used to live in this castle?" Zoe whispered.

"I guess so," I whispered back. I pointed to the door. "How do we get in there?"

"Who cares," Zoe said, her voice trembling. "Did you hear that?"

Nice beard :)

"Hear what?" I asked.

"THAT!" she said.

At that moment, I heard something that sounded a bit like a gush of wind and a bit like someone's voice. I couldn't make out what it said, but then the voice spoke again...

"Only by truth will you enter..."

The voice didn't sound human. It didn't even sound alive. I've heard the groaning of Egyptian mummies before and the voice on the staircase sounded just like that. No way I was hanging around to meet the undead – not without better Adventuring tools in my pocket!

We heard it again. "The truth!"

"OK, let's go," I said nervously, nearly bashing into Zoe as I turned around and headed back down the staircase.

The voice spoke again, louder this time, like it was following us. "Only by truth..."

As the voice became louder, I could hear the

sound of clanking metal coming towards us. It sounded like a knight in chain mail marching along.

By the time Zoe and I were at the bottom of the staircase, we were running for our lives.

We ran straight into a man.

"Arrrrrrhhhhhh!" we both screamed at the top of our lungs.

The man put a bony finger over his lips and glared at us through squinted eyes.

"Don't go shouting, you'll wake them..." he growled. He was tall and thin with grey hair and a blue blazer on. His face was drawn and he had dark circles under his eyes.

"Wake who? We're miles away from the dormitories," I said, trying not to sound seriously freaked out.

The man smiled knowingly. "I'm not worried

about waking the living. I'm worried about waking the dead!"

"OK," said Zoe, her voice shaking manically. "Well, we'll be getting back to bed then..."

"Wait!" said the man.

"Who are you?" I asked.

"My name's Jonas," he replied. "I'm the caretaker of Avalon Castle. As was my father, my father's father and his father before that. It's not just the castle I care for, but I care for its secrets too."

"Why are you telling us this?" I asked suspiciously. I felt Zoe glare at me. I knew she'd rather be running away from this guy at the speed of lightning rather than sticking around to find out who he was. But I'm an Adventurer, and it's my job to ask questions, even if I'm afraid what the answer might be.

"I saw you arrive," he said to me. "I saw that around your neck." He pointed at my amulet.

I reached down and grabbed my amulet tightly, tucking it back beneath my T-shirt.

"So what?" I shrugged.

"Come with me," he said.

"I think we'd rather..." Zoe started.

"OK," I said, cutting her off. She gave me a look that told me she'd fry my guts up with onions if she could.

Jonas walked off, and I tugged Zoe's arm and started following him. We walked behind him and he led us to a corridor that Zoe and I hadn't explored yet. Jonas stopped and stared up at a large picture of three knights. The knights were all holding swords and had metal helmets on their heads, hiding their faces.

I heard my name being screeched louder than a jet plane revving its engines.

Mrs Jones.

She was storming down the corridor towards us.

"What are you doing out of bed at this time, and Zoe, I am deeply disappointed in you!"

I turned around, looking for Jonas to get us out of trouble, but he was nowhere in sight.

Mrs Jones grabbed my arm tightly and marched us back to our rooms. "We'll discuss this in the morning!" she said angrily.

She didn't even give me a chance to say goodnight to Zoe – she literally threw me into the dorm!

I thought about what Jonas had said. What was the Talisman of Truth? Were the knights still looking for it? Could the castle really be haunted?

I took out my SurfM8 and typed away:

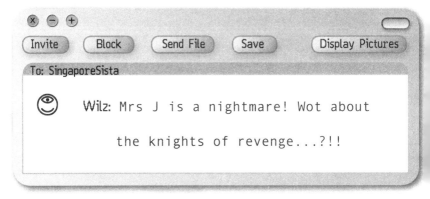

Zoe didn't IM back. But she had always, always IM'd back before...

44-04!

I was one of the first people down at breakfast the next morning. I was keen to see Zoe and talk to her about what Jonas had said the night before. Perhaps the Knights of Revenge had something to do with my Adventure? Perhaps I was meant to find that Talisman he was going on about?

Breakfast was being served in a large hall, a lot like the one I was sleeping in. There were coats of arms, tapestries and pictures on the walls. The room was filled with wooden benches around long wooden tables. I saved a seat for Zoe.

One by one, all the other kids in my class

appeared for breakfast. Mrs Jones came in with Jonas and seemed to be having a serious discussion with him. I have to admit, I was slightly relieved that Jonas was real. After the way he'd disappeared the night before, I had half convinced myself that I'd imagined him.

Soon everyone in my class was sitting down eating breakfast, apart from Zoe.

Weird.

I finished the last of my toast and headed towards Gemma Fletcher, a really tall, really clever, really goody-good-good girl in my class.

"Hey, Gemma," I said. Gemma stopped talking to her friends and looked up at me as if I'd just vomited on her breakfast. "You seen Zoe this morning?" I asked.

"No," she replied, looking embarrassed that she was talking to me. "She wasn't in her bed this morning."

"What?"

"Don't think she even slept in her bed – didn't look slept in if you ask me."

"Will Solvit!" Mrs Jones's voice bellowed across the hall. I turned around to see dozens of heads turned towards me. "Come with me," Mrs Jones demanded, as she walked out of the room.

I had no choice but to follow her – I guessed she wanted to speak to me about Zoe.

Jonas was waiting outside the breakfast hall.

"I want you to tell me the truth, Will," Mrs Jones said. She didn't sound angry or mad, just a bit worried, which made me start to worry. "Where's Zoe?"

"I don't know," I said, truthfully. "Last time I saw her was when you made us go to bed."

A worried frown wrinkled Mrs Jones's brow.

"Let's do one more search of the grounds before we call the school," she said to Jonas. He nodded his head at her and she marched off down the corridor without another word.

"What's going on?" I asked Jonas with concern.

"The Knights have taken their revenge!" he said in a growl. "I'll cover this up for your teachers, but it's up to you to find your friend." He took a step back and studied me with his tired eyes. "I knew as soon as you turned up that you were what the Knights of Revenge have been waiting for."

Excuse me???

The next thing I knew, Mr Mills, our history teacher, was rounding everyone up and taking us to a small room with school desks and chairs in it. I didn't get a chance to speak to Jonas or ask him what he was talking about.

The rest of the day passed in a blur. The last thing I could do was concentrate on history lessons and dumb walks around the castle grounds – there was too much else to think about:

- Where had Zoe gone to?
- How was I meant to find her?
- Who were the Knights of Revenge?
- What was the Talisman of Truth?
- How did I know that Jonas could be trusted?

It was getting dark outside and we came back into the castle from our walk around the grounds. That's when I spotted an envelope with my name on it sitting on the stone floor.

WHERE DO GHOSTS MAIL THEIR LETTERS?
AT THE GHOST OFFICE!

JONAS WAS RIGHT. ZOE HAS BEEN TAKEN BY
THE KNIGHTS OF REVENGE. SHE'S NOWHERE
MRS JONES, JONAS OR ANYONE ELSE CAN FIND
HER — ANYONE ELSE, THAT IS, APART FROM YOU.

TONIGHT YOU'LL HAVE A VISITOR. HE'LL GIVE YOU
A CLUE TO FINDING ZOE.

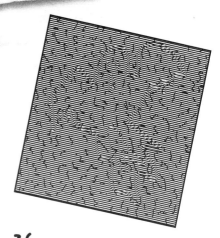

That night couldn't come quick enough. I don't remember eating dinner, brushing my teeth or getting ready for bed, but before I knew it I was under the covers and lying awake in the darkness. No one had said anything about Zoe, so I could only guess how worried Mrs Jones was, let alone Zoe's mum if she'd found out Zoe had gone missing.

I was lying in bed thinking when a light at the foot of my bed caught my eye. I looked up and couldn't believe what I saw.

There was a knight at the end of my bed. He looked just like the knights in the picture Jonas had taken us to – a Knight of Revenge. The knight didn't look solid, like a person does. If I squinted hard enough, I could see straight through him. I was in no doubt at all that the knight standing in front of me was a ghost.

"What has led you here?" asked a ghostly voice. It sounded just like the voice Zoe and I had heard on the staircase the night before.

"Um...a school trip," I answered, trying to sound brave.

"The truth has led you here," the ghost replied.

"Where's Zoe?" I asked, feeling braver this time.

"The girl will lead us to the truth."

"No, she won't," I said, feeling angry. "Zoe doesn't know anything. Let her go!"

"Come back and find her. We've waited so long for the truth."

"Where can I find you?" I asked with panic in my voice. The ghost was starting to disappear; I didn't want him to vanish before I found out where Zoe was.

"Find me at the court of Lord Avalon..." was all

he said before he vanished into thin air.

Great. So now I knew for sure that my best friend had been kidnapped by a ghostly order of ancient knights. I guessed that finding Zoe had something to do with time travel. It was my special Adventuring skill after all. But how did I know where to time travel to?

I whipped Morph out of my bag and quickly programmed it to become a computer. Morph is this cool invention of my dad's that can turn into just about anything if you've got the right memory chip. I logged onto the internet and typed 'Court of Avalon' into the search engine.

This is what came up:

Lord Avalon lived in the historic Avalon Castle from 1103–1179. He held court at his castle every summer.

I searched the internet for ages but couldn't find any other details about the Court of Avalon. The only choice I had was to fire Morph up in to a time machine, get in and hope for the best. Morph has a clever way of taking me where I need to go.

I didn't waste another minute. Without even stopping to put on my shoes, pack Adventure tools or change out of my pyjamas, I revved Morph into a time machine and was stepping inside.

"Take me where I need to go, Morph," I said hopefully. "Take me to Zoe." The time machine door slammed closed and I began to feel myself whizzing back through time.

CHAPTER FOUR
MEDIEVAL SMELLS = TOTAL STINK-VILLE

One thing you should know about travelling back in time is that most places in the past STINK worse than dino dung! As soon as the time machine door swung open, I was trying not to puke in my mouth – the stench around me was so bad! Rotten eggs, piles of cow pats, mouldy vegetables, sweaty armpits and teeth before the invention of toothbrushes – bad combination, trust me!

I tried to breathe through my mouth as I got used to the smell, deactivating Morph and putting the shrunk-down version into my pocket.

Looking around me, I could tell I was in the

castle courtyard. The castle battlements and the drawbridge over the moat were behind me and the main castle was in front of me. People were coming over the drawbridge and into the castle courtyard, pulling wagons stacked high with vegetables.

The castle itself looked the same as it did in modern times, only there were flags hanging out of windows and stains on the castle walls where people had thrown buckets of poo out of the windows on to the ground below.

The ground beneath my feet was muddy, not like the perfect grass that surrounded the castle in the present – certainly no 'Keep Off the Grass' signs back in the olden days!

An old woman pushing a cart of cabbages barged into me and nearly knocked me over. "Cabbage to cure warts, boy?" she asked.

"Excuse me?"

"Warts, this magic cabbage can cure 'em!" She needed some cabbage action herself – big time! Her whole face was covered with warts, and she looked worse than a lumpy toad.

"Er, no thanks," I said, as politely as I could.

The old woman shrugged and carried on, pushing her cabbage cart through the mud and muttering under her breath.

I must have been too busy looking at all the crazy sights around me, because I hadn't moved since I arrived. I must have been standing there for ages.

"You selling anything?" said a man behind me.

I turned around and saw a middle-aged man wearing a blue cap and colourful clothes.

43

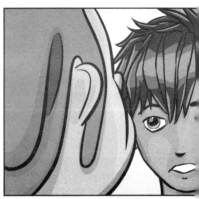

How was I meant to get out of this one? I was locked into stocks and about to get pelted with rotten veg!

"Release him!" shouted a voice from the back of the crowd.

Suddenly the crowd hushed to silence and then began to whisper among themselves.

"Silence!" called the voice again.

I recognized that voice. I'd recognize it anywhere – Zoe.

From my stocks I could see the crowds of market goers begin to part, and a group of knights walked towards me. The knights were dressed head to toe in gleaming silver armour, in their hands they carried sharp spears and around their waists hung heavy-looking swords. They were all wearing white tabards with the symbol of my amulet on them.

The Knights of Revenge.

Zoe was standing in the middle of the group of knights. Only she didn't look like the Zoe I knew – she was dressed like some kind of medieval princess. She was wearing a long pink dress and had a silly headdress on her head.

Funny dress!

"Zoe?" I shouted at her. "Let me out of here, will you?"

"Release him," she instructed the knights.

One of the knights headed towards me and began unlocking the stocks.

"Thanks," I began.

"Now take him away and lock him in the castle jail!" Zoe ordered.

WHAT?

"Zoe, it's me, Will!" I said in disbelief. Why was she pretending she didn't know me? How could she do this to me?

"I don't know who he is," she said. I could tell that she was lying – but why?

I knew that Zoe wouldn't let a bunch of knights with swords lock me up without a reason. I figured she had a plan. So I played along.

I let the knights march me away from the market, the peasants glaring at me as if I was some kind of criminal.

Thcy lcd me into the castle. It was just like it was in modern times, only smellier and dirtier. The paintings on the wall were bright and looked brand new, not old and faded like they did in the present.

The knights led me to a staircase that took us in to dark, damp cellars. We walked through a dim tunnel lit by torch light.

At some point Zoe must have stopped walking with us because I was alone with the knights. I started to feel uneasy about the fact she'd abandoned me – I tried to remind myself that this must all be part of her plan.

The knights led me into a corridor lined with jail cells. In the dim torch light I could just about make out the prisoners being held captive. Some of them were tied up and some of them were clinging to the bars, begging to be let out. They all looked as if they were starving and as if they hadn't seen daylight for years.

A shudder ran down my spine as we arrived at an empty cell. The knights unlocked it and threw me in.

I fell to the cold jail cell floor with a thud. I felt a rat scuttle over my feet as I heard the jail door slam shut, locking me in.

The knights walked off without another word, leaving me alone in the cell with nothing but rats and the screams of other prisoners for company.

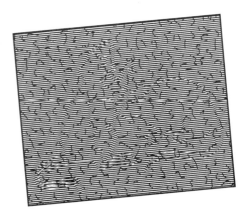

Something in the flickering torch light caught my eye. It was a square of white paper perched up against the wall of my jail cell.

A letter.

There was a hungry rat nibbling the corner of the envelope. Before the rat could make a meal of it, I picked up the letter and quickly read what it had to say.

HOW DO YOU KNOW WHEN A RAT IS HUNGRY?
HE'S BREATHING!

DON'T BE ALARMED — YOU'RE WHERE YOU NEED TO BE. SOON YOU'LL HAVE TO GAIN THE TRUST OF THE KNIGHTS.

FOLLOW THESE CLUES TO PREPARE YOURSELF FOR WHAT IS AHEAD.

THIS BEAST HAS SCALES AND CAN
BREATHE FLAME,
YOU CANNOT WIN THE FIGHT SO
THEIR WILL YOU MUST TAME.

Beast that has scales and breathes fire = dragons!

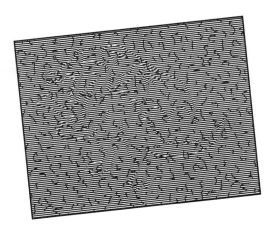

Most people might think that dragons don't exist – but most people also think that time travel's impossible, and I know differently.

But I didn't understand what the clue in the letter was telling me to do. How could I prepare for a fight with a dragon that I couldn't win? And how on earth can you tame a dragon?

Alone in my jail cell, I didn't have much else to do apart from think about what the clue in my letter meant.

- Maybe I had to let the dragon kill me?
- Maybe I had to tame the dragon with food?
- Can dragons speak English?
- Did Zoe know about this whole dragon fight thing?
- Why was Zoe letting the Knights of Revenge lock me up in a rat-infested cell?

I had been in the cell for hours and was nearly falling asleep next to the rats when I heard the clank of metal armour charging towards me.

"Will?" said a knight. I couldn't see his face. It was covered by a helmet.

"Yeah?" I replied, standing up hopefully.

"We've come to take you away," he said. "The Lady Zoe wishes to speak with you."

He unlocked the heavy jail door and swung it open.

A knight stood on either side of me as we walked back through the dark, damp jail. The sounds of prisoners screaming rung in my ears as we walked. It was awful!

Without a word, I was marched up into the

Squeak!

54

main castle, through the vast corridors and to the hall that I'd had breakfast in that morning.

Grand wooden doors to the hall swung open, and inside was a large throne. The walls of the great hall were lined with tapestries – they looked really bright, not as faded as they did in modern times. Zoe was sitting on the throne and there were two knights on either side of her.

I walked up to Zoe and one of the knights at my side forced me down onto my knees. "Bow before the Lady!" he ordered.

"OK, OK," I said, bowing my head to Zoe.

A mischievous smile crept across Zoe's face – she was enjoying this a bit too much!

"Leave us!" she commanded. The knights who had led me in and the ones who were standing by her side all bowed slightly before walking away, closing the hall doors and leaving us alone.

"What in the name of the Partek is going on?" I asked.

Zoe leapt off her throne and flung her arms around me. "Oh, Will, I'm so glad you're here."

"Of course I was going to come and find you, silly," I said, pushing her off. "You belong in the 21st century – not here."

"Will, we don't have much time so I have to be quick," she said with worry in her voice.

"Fire away," I said, eager for her to tell me what was going on.

"Did you bring your amulet with you?" she asked with concern.

"This amulet?" I said, pulling out my amulet from under my T-shirt. She nodded at the sight of it. "Of course," I smiled. "I never take it off."

"Listen," she said. "That night we explored the castle and Mrs Jones found us and sent us back to bed… As I was walking back into my dormitory the ghost of a knight blocked my path. It said it had come to capture me because I would lead the knights to the Talisman of Truth…"

"What is this Talisman everyone's going on about…"

"Will, don't interrupt," she scolded.

"Sorry."

"Before I knew it, they'd somehow brought me back here – don't ask me how, it all happened too quickly. They've been treating me like some kind of princess. They think I'm special because I can lead them to the Talisman. They told me that the Talisman of Truth is the most powerful object ever created by mankind. It shows the wearer the truth – but not just anyone can wear it…"

"Who wears it? How are you meant to lead the

knights to the Talisman?" I asked eagerly.

Shame blushed over Zoe's face and guilt flooded her eyes. "I just did, Will," she said quietly. "I led them to you."

Before I knew it, the tapestries on the wall started to move and the Knights of Revenge revealed themselves – they'd been hiding behind the tapestries the whole time I'd been speaking to Zoe.

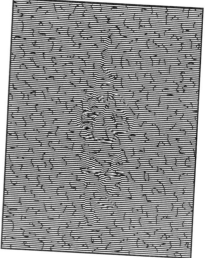

They charged towards me, their swords drawn and pointing.

"You promised you wouldn't hurt him," Zoe

screamed as the knights rushed towards me.

"What's going on?" I shouted, too confused to understand what was happening.

I felt the weight of a knight's arm push me to the ground, and a metallic glove pulled at the amulet around my neck, ripping the cord that held it in place.

The knight who'd ripped off my amulet held it up triumphantly and declared, "At last, the Talisman of Truth!"

"What was it doing with a boy?" another knight asked, his voice gruff and low. "We've sworn to search for the Talisman until the end of time and we find it around the neck of a boy!"

"Bring him to Lord Avalon, and bring the girl too," the first knight ordered.

I felt someone pull me to my feet and push me towards the door.

What is going on?

"Will, I'm sorry," Zoe said, looking like she was going to cry.

"It's OK," I told her. I didn't know who this Lord Avalon was, or what the Talisman of Truth was, but one thing I did know for certain was that I needed to get my amulet back!

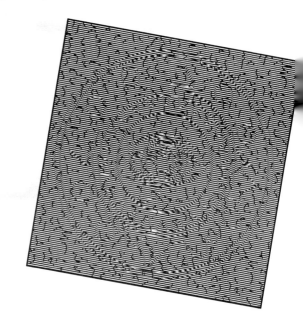

Close your eyes and imagine a wizard's study...
imagine the smell of cauldron smoke, spicy
herbs and dirty animals. Imagine the sounds
of bubbling potions, crackling flames and the
scuttle of insects in jars. Imagine layers of thick
dust on spell books and piles and piles of books

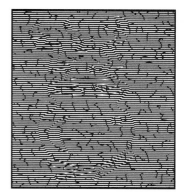

everywhere you look.
Well, imagine this is
how Lord Avalon's room
looked.

The room itself was
at the top of a narrow
staircase – the staircase

that Zoe and I had explored just before we met Jonas. Lord Avalon's room was the room that had no lock and no handle. This time the door was open when we got to the top of the staircase.

Lord Avalon was sitting in a chair with his back to us when we entered the room. One of the knights coughed loudly and Lord Avalon slowly got to his feet and turned around to look at us.

He had long grey hair and

a beard that was twiddled into little dreadlocks. He was wearing a dark blue cloak that looked like the colour of deep water. I recognized him straight away as the man in the picture on the top of the staircase.

"This BOY was wearing the Talisman," said the knight standing behind me.

"Is that so, Barnaby," the Lord Avalon said softly.

"He is only a boy, my Lord," Barnaby the knight replied. "Clearly an imposter. Shall we torture him so he tells us who the true owner is?"

I gulped hard at the word 'torture'.

"No, Barnaby," the Lord Avalon said calmly, "I don't think torture is a good idea."

"Me neither," I said loudly.

"Will, be quiet," Zoe begged.

"I won't be quiet," I argued with her, "I want

63

my amulet back."

The knight behind me tossed my amulet through the air and Lord Avalon caught it in his hand. "Your amulet?" he smiled at me. "It is my amulet now."

"What do you want with it?" I asked Lord Avalon.

"Silence!" said one of the knights.

Lord Avalon waved his hand, telling the knight to be quiet. "The young man is simply curious. Isn't that right?" he asked me.

I slowly nodded my head in agreement.

"I am Lord Avalon, and the Lord of this castle," he told me. "I command an order of brave knights whose sole purpose is to search for this small object here in my hand." He held my amulet up to the moonlight pouring through a window. It glistened and glinted in the light.

WILL'S FACT FILE

Dear Adventurer,

Even though fairytale castles sound nice enough, the Middle Ages was one of the bloodiest periods in history. Did you know that the Medieval Church thought it was OK to rip out a person's toenails? Or that when holy people died their bodies were chopped up and the bits sold off as 'relics'?

Read lots of other cool and disturbing facts and then amaze your family and friends with your incredible knowledge.

Did you know? During the Middle Ages Marco Polo made a mammoth journey from Italy to China!

Timeline

1066
William the Conqueror invades England.

1078
The Tower of London is built.

1085
The Domesday Book records all people and property in England.

1170
Thomas Becket is murdered in Canterbury Cathedral.

1184
The Church starts a series of Inquisitions against so-called heretics.

1212
The Children's Crusade is l[e...] by a 12-year-old French bo[y...]

1215
King John of England signs the Magna Carta.

1271
The Last Crusade sets out.

1348-50
The Black Death ravages Europe.

1377-1453
Hundred Years War is fough[t...] between France and Englar[d...]

1381
Peasants' Revolt in England is put down.

1415
Battle of Agincourt (part of Hundred Years W[ar...])

1431
Capture, trial and execution of Joan of Arc.

1478
The Spanish Inquisition is established.

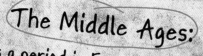

The Middle Ages:

- is a period in European history.
- roughly refers to the 5th to 16th centuries.
- saw the rise of the knight and stone castles.
- saw much of Europe dominated by the Roman Catholic Church.
- saw a lot of religious persecution.
- was a time of bloody wars, many in the name of God.
- started with the fall of the Roman Empire.
- ended with the Italian Renaissance (a period of great cultural change).

DID YOU KNOW...

Medieval is the adjective for the Middle Ages.

In the Middle Ages, society was organized into the '**feudal system**', which was based on owning land.
- The king was at the top of society.
- Below him were the nobles.
- The knights were given land in return for military service.
- Most of the population was made up of peasants. They worked the land and had very few rights.

William the Conqueror introduced the feudal system into England.

Kings thought they could do anything and could be pretty cruel.
- A king could barge into any house and take whatever he wanted.
- King Peter of Spain was so bad, he was nicknamed Peter the Cruel.
- William II of England was mysteriously killed by an arrow in the New Forest.

King John signed the Magna Carta, limiting the king's power in England.

The **nobles** ran things for the king.
- They collected taxes, settled legal issues and led an army of knights
- Nobles lived in castles.
- When they weren't at war, nob spent most of their time hunti
- They dined well on everythi from pork and venison to sw
- Noblewomen had no rights

Nobles enjoyed fine banquets with entertainment from jesters.

Knights were soldiers and gentlemen.
· Knights rode into battle on horses, wearing heavy armour.
· A trainee knight was called a squire.
· A squire served a knight until he became one around age 16.
· Before a boy became a squire, he served as a page boy.

Knights fought with lances, swords and axes.

Knights had to fight like gentlemen.

A knight's behaviour was supposed to follow a **code of chivalry**.
· Knights were supposed to defend the poor, women and children.
· They had to obey and defend the Church.
· They should always be brave, kind, generous and humble.
· Above all they had to serve their lord, king and country.

Knights practised fighting at **tournaments**.
· They fought in mock battles.
· Swordfights were also popular.
· Although blunt weapons were used, knights were still killed.
· The prize was money and the loser's armour and horse.
· Tournaments started in France.

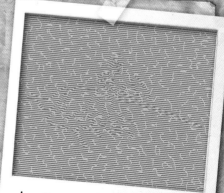

Jousting was a tournament event.

Life was very tough for **peasants** at the bottom of society.
· By law, peasants (or serfs) didn't even belong to themselves.
· They had to pay unfair taxes.
· Peasants worked the land, made goods or served lords.
· Peasants shared one-roomed huts with pigs and other animals.
· Most peasants only lived to 25!

For breakfast peasants might eat bread crust washed down with beer!

The Church was very powerful and dominated everyone's lives.
· The Catholic Church was the only religion in Europe.
· The Church had its own laws, lands and taxes.
· The Church collected 10 per cent of what every peasant produced.
· Non-Christians were often treated badly, or even killed.

Every village had a church — you could be punished if you didn't go!

The Church called anyone who disagreed with it a '**heretic**'.
· Heretics were put on trial in secret by bishops.
· At the trials the accused could be tortured if no blood was shed.
· Under torture victims would confess to almost anything.
· Most people tried were found guilty — even if they weren'

The guilty could be put in prison or even burnt at the stake.

The Crusades: Between 1095 and 1291 Christian Europe declared war on Muslims in the Holy Land.
The Pope encouraged these wars. At first, the wars were to get Jerusalem back from the Turks. People saw them as a religious pilgrimage, but they were very bloody, with men seeking glory.
The Crusades were led by kings, nobles and knights.

There were nine crusades in total.

Most castles had a drawbridge and a moat.

Rich barons and knights lived in strongly defended **castles**.
- Early castles were built of wood but they were easily burnt down.
- After 1066 builders used stone.
- Castles were like small towns, with carpenters, blacksmiths and more.
- Few castles had a dungeon but most had a torture chamber.

Torture was a popular way to punish people or make them confess.
Thumbscrews were used to crush thumbs, fingers or even toes.
The rack was used to stretch people until bones were dislocated or even limbs ripped off.
Women accused of witchcraft were dunked into freezing water.

The iron maiden was a coffin lined with sharp spikes.

Naughty children had their fingers trapped in the finger pillory.

Childhood was very short. Many children died young, and many of those who didn't had to work.
· Very few children went to schoo
· Poorer children worked in the fields from about the age of 7.
· Noble children were sometimes given to monasteries or abbeys.
· Some noble children were taug at home by tutors.

Deadly **illnesses** were a part of daily life.
· Living conditions were often filthy and crowded.
· Cures were bizarre and often downright dangerous.
· The Church taught that illness was a punishment from God.
· The average medieval person could expect to live to 36 or 37.

Attaching blood-sucking leeches to flesh was a popular cure.

In 1348 a great plague nam **the Black Death** hit Europe
· 1/3 of the population died
· Symptoms included lumps under the arms and black sp
· There was no cure.
· The Black Death is also known as the Bubonic Plagu

The plague was spread by the fleas carried by black rats.

"We're from the future," Zoe said. I rolled my eyes – Zoe always gives us away. She's a rubbish Adventure companion sometimes!

"I know…" said the Lord Avalon.

"You do?" I replied in shock. "How?"

"Because I was the one who put a curse on the souls of these good knights," he said, pointing to the knights around us. "I was the person who kept their spirits here on Earth long after they died so that they could one day bring you to me."

"You turned the knights into ghosts?" Zoe asked.

"Yes," he replied.

"Why was it so important that you brought us here?" I asked curiously.

He stared at me thoughtfully and stayed quiet for a while before he spoke. "How much do you know about this?" he asked, holding up my amulet.

"I know that it's mine and that you took it from me," I answered angrily.

"But do you know what power it possesses?" he asked.

"Just tell them, Will," Zoe said shrugging.

"It can open locks," I admitted. "And it helps me understand other languages."

A loud gasp echoed around the stone room.

"The wearer of Truth cannot be a boy!" shouted one knight in disbelief.

"You are the Master of Time?" said the Lord Avalon.

"How did you know that?" I asked quietly, stunned that he knew the Adventurer nickname that the ancient Aztecs had given me.

"The signs told me that it would be you, although they did not say how young you'd be."

"Signs?" Zoe asked.

"Yes, in my spells," he replied. "The Master of Time is the greatest Adventurer that ever lived. But he does not realize this yet, and he does not know why he will go on to possess this title."

"'The greatest Adventurer that ever lived'?" I asked in amusement, not believing a word Lord Avalon was saying. "What makes you say that?"

Lord Avalon smiled at me.

"I don't believe this boy is who he says he is," said Barnaby the knight bitterly.

"Don't worry," said Lord Avalon. "If he really is the Master of Time and the greatest Adventurer that ever lived, then he'll be able to help us with our current quest."

"The dragon!" said Barnaby loudly. "He's here to kill the dragon!"

"Dragon?" gasped Zoe.

"The dragon has been terrorizing the villages of Avalon," said Barnaby. "Killing the dragon was our next mission of revenge!"

"Yes," said Lord Avalon. "If anyone can help us solve our dragon problem, then it's this boy here. If he succeeds, then we'll let him live."

"And if I don't succeed?" I asked with worry.

Lord Avalon smiled. "You won't live to tell the tale."

So this is what the letter meant. I have to gain their trust and prove who I am by meeting this dragon.

Lord Avalon threw my amulet back to Barnaby before turning around and sitting down with his back to us. I felt Barnaby's heavy hand press down on my shoulder as he began to steer me out of Lord Avalon's room.

"Guard the Talisman. Take them into the

forest," Lord Avalon called as the knights began to march Zoe and me down the staircase. "Find the dragon that has caused us so many problems. Slay it and bring me back its head!"

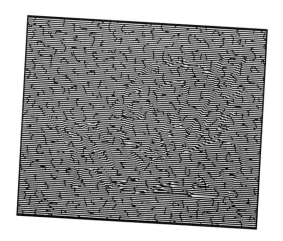

CHAPTER SEVEN
THE JOUST

So that's how Zoe and I ended up travelling through a medieval forest with the Knights of Revenge. We were off in search of a deadly dragon that had been causing havoc in the nearby villages. And I was somehow meant to confront this dragon and stop it killing people so that I could prove to the knights that I was really a Time Travelling Adventurer.

Normally, taking on a dragon wouldn't worry me at all. But normally, I have a bag full of awesome Adventure tools to help me fight. I'd been in such a rush to rescue Zoe that I hadn't packed anything to help me on my Adventure before travelling back in time.

At least I had Morph. But I couldn't work out how Morph could help me defeat a dragon – unless I turned it into a jet plane and flew as far away as I could.

I needed my amulet back. I was starting to think that maybe the amulet had powers that I hadn't discovered yet – why else would Lord Avalon and the Knights of Revenge make such a fuss about it? I didn't even know why people kept calling it the 'Talisman of Truth'.

One thing I did know is that I needed the amulet back.

"So, this Talisman," I asked Barnaby the knight as he beat his way through the forest thicket on his horse. "Why do you call it the Talisman of Truth?"

"If you don't know that," said another knight, "then you certainly aren't the rightful owner." I sighed.

Zoe and I were sharing a horse. I was at the front and she was sitting behind me. She was still wearing her stupid medieval princess outfit and I was still wearing my pyjamas. Not the best clothes for Adventuring – trust me.

We were travelling through the forest with four of the Knights of Revenge. They each had their own horse. They didn't have to share.

The leader of the group of knights seemed to be Barnaby. Then there was another guy they kept calling Bert, another called Jack and one called Peter. I couldn't tell them apart unless they spoke – they were all wearing identical silver armour and didn't once lift their metal helmets up so I could see their faces.

"So this...dragon..." Zoe said nervously. "Why exactly do you want to get revenge on it?"

"We're the Knights of Revenge," replied Jack. "Revenge is what we do best."

"We were selected by Lord Avalon for being the bravest, wisest, most loyal knights in the whole Kingdom," said Bert. "Only knights like us can seek revenge and protect the Talisman of Truth."

"So what has this dragon done that's so bad?" I asked.

"He's a dragon..." Peter said simply. "It's his very nature to destroy and kill. We seek revenge for that which he has destroyed and those that he has killed."

"Dragons have long been a great threat to us," Barnaby explained as our horses climbed up a muddy bank in the forest. "They live in caves by the mountains, but when they leave the caves they come to our villages and set alight houses with their fiery breath. This latest dragon has caused a lot of damage and many people have been harmed."

"So let me get this right," Zoe said. "You want Will to kill this dragon, and if he does, you'll believe he's a Time Travelling Adventurer and give him back his amulet?"

"If he can kill the beast, without a sword, without any weapon at all…" Bert chuckled beneath his helmet.

"But that's impossible!" Zoe shouted in my ear, so loudly that she startled the horse we were riding on.

"It's OK," I said quietly, turning around to look at her. "I'm not going to kill it, I'm going to tame it."

"Will, have you gone mad?" she whispered back. "You can't tame a dragon. It'll barbecue you before you even try!"

"Night is fast approaching," announced Barnaby. He pointed to a clearing in the forest. "We shall camp here tonight."

Everyone dismounted their horses and tied them to trees. It was getting mega dark and owls were beginning to hoot around us.

"So, tell me," said Barnaby, as he began to gather wood to build a fire. "Why do you think we should trust you, a child?"

"I'm the only one here. If an adult had shown up wearing the amulet then you'd trust him." I always thought knights were pretty cool, but they're not. Not these knights anyway – they're moody and rude and arrogant. "Besides," I snapped, "just because I'm a child doesn't mean I couldn't beat any of you guys in a fight."

"Oh really…" challenged Barnaby.

"Don't, he's only a child…" laughed Bert. "We don't want him dead before we reach the dragon's cave."

"No," I argued. "Give me a chance to prove myself!"

Barnaby put down the firewood he was holding and turned towards me. I wished I could see under his helmet – without seeing his face I had no idea what he was thinking.

"Very well," Barnaby said. "You may prove yourself in a fight with me. But I will choose the method of fighting."

"Fine," I said confidently. I was mega sure that Barnaby would choose sword fighting, and I was ace with a sword – I'd had loads of practice. "If I win," I said, "then you give me my amulet back."

There was silence as everyone looked at Barnaby, waiting for him to speak. He nodded his head in agreement. "And if you lose," he said, "then I keep the amulet and I kill you and your friend right here tonight – then this silly quest can stop wasting my time. There's no way you are who you say you are – you're just a boy."

"I'm not just a boy," I said angrily. "I'm an Adventurer, and I'm going to prove it to you."

"Bert!" Barnaby shouted. "Prepare the horses for a joust!"

A joust! *Uh-oh!*

A joust was not part of my plan. Just in case you were wondering, a joust is when two people ride horses and charge at each other with long poles. Whoever falls off their horse first loses.

"You can't joust," Zoe said loudly – I could see by the panic in her eyes that she was trying to get me out of this. "You don't have a lance."

"We're in a forest," laughed Barnaby. "We have hundreds of trees that we can use as lances."

Great – so there was no way I was getting out of the joust. I'd never jousted before. I didn't even know the rules. Plus, it was hardly fair – Barnaby was wearing a suit of armour and I was wearing pyjamas!

Before I knew it, Pete had used two fallen tree branches to create lances for me and Barnaby to joust with.

Barnaby climbed on to his large, powerful horse. Zoe gave me a leg-up so I could sit on the back of our horse, who was exhausted from the long journey that day.

My heart was racing as my horse backed up and faced Barnaby's horse. Barnaby sat on his horse like a king – he was so confident, he must have jousted a million times.

When the flag waves, we charge.

Be careful, Will!

Barnaby came at me fast.

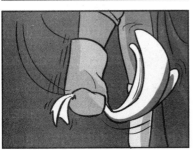

I ducked and pointed my lance at his chest.

Barnaby fell to the ground with a THUD.

I had won!

Nice work, Adventurer!

High five!

So, do you believe who I am now?

"Not until you've defeated the dragon," he growled at me.

"But you have to give Will his amulet back," said Zoe sternly. "You promised, remember."

Without a word, Barnaby stood up and pulled my amulet out from under his armour. He handed it to me.

Result!

I had my amulet back.

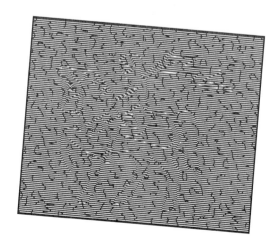

CHAPTER EIGHT
DRAGON MOUNTAIN

I was woken up the next morning by the smell of sausages. Barnaby and the other Knights of Revenge were cooking on the fire.

"Breakfast?" Barnaby asked.

He didn't need to ask twice – I was STARVING!

I scoffed down five whole sausages, and Zoe ate four. They were the tastiest five sausages I've ever had – trekking through a medieval forest and jousting with knights makes you really hungry!

"We're only a couple of hours' walk away from the dragon's lair," Pete the knight informed us

83 Mmmmmm!

calmly.

I was starting to feel a bit panicked about the whole dragon thing. I hadn't worked out what I was meant to do when we finally came face to face. The letter had already told me that fighting wouldn't work, but I still couldn't understand how I was meant to tame a dragon.

After breakfast, we packed up the camp, climbed onto the horses and started moving.

Within two hours, we'd arrived at a large cave in the mountainside.

"We're here," announced Barnaby. "Dragon Mountain."

He turned around to face me. "You'll be going in to the cave alone. Bring out the beast dead."

I've faced some pretty stomach-flippingly scary creatures throughout my Adventures, but I'd never met a dragon – until now!

Usually, when I come face to face with my enemies, I have my Adventurer tools to help me fight them. But all I had walking into the cave were my tattered pyjamas and my amulet – or the 'Talisman of Truth' as the knights kept calling it. But I couldn't see how that was meant to help me, unless there was a door I had to unlock and run away through!

"Good luck, Will," Zoe said with a brave smile on her face. "You can do it. I'll be waiting here for you."

I took a deep breath and started walking into the cave in the mountainside.

The cave was dark – pitch black. At first it was quiet, but then I began to hear noises.

HUFF PUFF HUFF

It was the dragon breathing.

I gulped hard, wishing I had something to help me fight: my stun gun, supersonic screecher, a sword – even a blunt pencil would be better than nothing!

When I time travelled back to ancient Roman times, the military general Mark Antony taught me the first rule of combat – to let your enemy think you're fearless, even if you're not.

I knew that if I was to have any chance of surviving this Adventure, I had to let the dragon know I meant business. I couldn't let the dragon get a whiff of my fear.

"I am Will Solvit," I shouted loudly, my voice echoing around the cave in the darkness. "I am the feared Master of Time. Show yourself to me!"

At that moment, I heard a small whimpering. It sounded more like a crying puppy than a dragon.

I started to wonder if this was all a wind-up, and if the knights had brought me out here to make fun of me, not to watch me battle a dragon.

"Show yourself!" I shouted once more.

The whimpering got louder…and louder.

I heard a scuffling. And suddenly, out of the shadows, waddled the most magnificent, terrifying beast I'd ever seen.

The dragon towered above me – he was easily the size of a three-storey house. His legs were as fat as tree trunks and even though his wings were tucked tightly into his side I could tell that once open, their span would be gigantic.

Suddenly, I didn't feel quite so confident.

The letter was right – there was no way I could win a fight with this thing.

The dragon let out a snotty snort and a splutter of snot and fire exploded from his nose.

I jumped backwards and tried not to scream.

The dragon was whimpering loudly.

Then something strange happened...I felt the amulet around my neck begin to glow and get warmer – the way it does when it starts to translate another language.

You won't believe what happened next...

"I'm so, so sorry," snivelled the dragon in a thick lisp.

I stayed silent, stunned at being spoken to by a dragon.

"I can't stop it – the fire, it just comes out," the dragon said, whimpering again and puffing little clouds of mega-hot steam from his nose.

"Did you just speak?" I asked him, astonished.

"You speak Dragon?" he asked, equally stunned.

"Er...no..." a light bulb flicked on inside my

head as I realized what was going on. "But my amulet does."

"You're here to help me?" the dragon said, hopefully. "That is why you can understand."

"Erm," I stuttered, not knowing quite what to say or do. "I guess so," I answered. "But you gotta promise not to blow flames at me if you want my help."

The dragon let out a loud wail and a huge puff of snot, flames and smoke shot from his nose. "I don't want to hurt you!" he sobbed.

"Calm down," I shouted back, trying to be calm myself.

"All I want is a friend," he wailed, tiny spurts of flame flickering from his nose as he spoke. "But every time I go near anyone, my nose shoots fire and I hurt people."

"Can't you control it?" I asked.

The dragon spluttered, "Control?"

"Hasn't another dragon shown you how to control your fire-breathing?"

"There are no other dragons around here," he sobbed pathetically. "I'm the only one…I'm so lonely!"

"OK, OK," I said, starting to realise that the dragon was no more a killer than I was a dancing bogey. "What's your name?" I asked, trying to sound friendly.

"Egbert," he lisped at me.

What kind of fruit loop names a dragon Egbert?

"OK, Egbert," I said, trying not to laugh when I said his name. "I'll help you. There must be a way for you to control your flames. We'll figure it out together."

"We can be friends?" he asked, coughing and spluttering snot and flames into the cave.

Charming!

"Yes," I replied. I quite liked the idea of having a dragon as a friend. "Well, I don't really live around here, but I can introduce you to people who do, and once they know you're not going to barbecue them, I'm sure they'd love to be your friend."

Egbert's mouth grinned into a scaly smile.

So that was that – no big battle, no killing or being killed. All Egbert needed was someone to understand him – someone to see the truth in the situation. I guess that's what the amulet helped me do.

I led Egbert out of the cave – making sure I was far enough ahead not to get burned if he had an accident.

You should have seen Zoe's face when I appeared out of the cave with a dragon waddling behind me! She looked like her eyes were going to pop out of her head and start doing a disco dance! Even the knights looked terrified – I couldn't see their faces but I could tell by the way they jumped up in the air with fright that they were shocked to see me with Egbert.

"Will…" Zoe said nervously. "What's going on?"

"It's OK," I explained. I told her and the knights all about Egbert wanting to be friends with them and about him wanting to learn how to control his flames.

"How do you know all this?" Barnaby asked in amazement.

"My amulet," I said simply.

At that moment, the four knights fell to their knees and bowed their heads at me.

"What are you doing?" I asked, confused.

"We doubted you," said Barnaby. "You really

are the Master of Time – the Talisman would show the truth to no other."

"That's what I've been telling you all along!" I said, slightly annoyed that we had to trek out to speak to a dragon for them to believe me.

"We must return to the castle at once," said Barnaby. "The Lord Avalon must be informed of the truth."

The knights mounted their horses, getting ready for the trip back.

"You're gonna have an extra horse on the journey," I said with a smile.

"Master?" said Barnaby.

I liked being called 'Master'.

"Zoe and I won't be travelling back by horse," I said simply. Zoe raised an eyebrow at me and I heard a delighted huff from Egbert. "We'll be flying on Egbert."

Egbert dutifully bowed down, lowering his body as close to the ground as he could. Zoe and I went round to climb onto him – she gave me a leg-up and then I helped pull her up to sit on Egbert's back with me.

"You know the way?" Egbert asked me.

Awesome!

"No," I replied. "But the Talisman of Truth will guide us."

Without another word to the gob-smacked knights below, Egbert shot up into the air and started soaring through the skies.

I was right about his wingspan – it was HUGE!

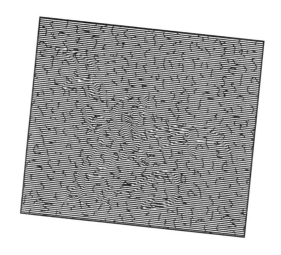

CHAPTER NINE
THE TALISMAN
OF TRUTH

I don't know if you know this or not – but Zoe
and I are both awesome with swords. We once
spent some time with a group of Japanese
samurais and they taught us everything they
knew when it comes to swordplay.

Obviously, being in medieval times,
surrounded by knights, was an excellent
opportunity to practise our sword skills. So
as soon as we were all back at the castle, the
knights were happy to fight with us and teach us
a few tricks of their own.

We stayed there, at the medieval castle, for a

few days. Now that the Knights of Revenge knew I wasn't lying about being an Adventurer, they were really cool to hang out with.

Zoe spent most of the day practising her sword skills with the knights, and when I wasn't joining in, I was either training Egbert or helping Barnaby write the very first Dragon/English dictionary. It was important they could understand Egbert when I left.

In case you were wondering, these are my favourite Dragon words:

- **Exxzhhhba** = Fart
- **Bzzhyburt** = Snot
- **Fallwzzka** = Burp
- **Mkkzzni** = Bum
- **Qvfra** = Friend

And these are my top five tips for taming a dragon:

- Reward them with treats of rotten cabbage (it's their favourite food)
- Always stay at least six metres from them (in case they accidentally toast you)
- Keep lessons short (dragons have very short attention spans)
- Ride them often (this helps them trust you, which helps them learn quicker)
- Give them lots of praise (dragons are very insecure creatures)

After three days of being back at the castle, I was finally summoned to speak to Lord Avalon. I was surprised he hadn't wanted to see me sooner, but I guess Lords are quite busy people.

"You're doing excellent work with Egbert," he told me, as I took a seat in his study. "I've only ever read of such achievements. I never believed it to be possible."

"I'm writing down everything I know about training dragons. Barnaby will be taking over when I go home," I told him.

"I didn't call you here to speak about dragons," Lord Avalon informed me. "I brought you here to talk about the Talisman of Truth."

"I was wondering when you were going to tell me about it," I said, intrigued by what he had to say.

He sat down opposite me, a desk with piles of dusty books between us.

"I'll start at the beginning," Lord Avalon said. He pushed some of the books aside so he had a better view of me. "The Talisman was forged in the first fire built by man."

"The first fire?" I asked.

"Yes, in the first fire that man ever made, they forged the Talisman. They created it so that their ancestors would always have a way to know the truth. The Talisman is as old as mankind itself, and is one of the most important tools ever created."

"I had no idea," I said honestly. "Why do I have it?"

"Because you are the true ancestor."

"So, the Solvit family were the first ever human beings? And I've descended from them?"

"I'm sure they went by different names back then, and I'm sure they looked quite different from you, Will," he smiled. "But, yes, you are a direct descendant of the first ever humans."

"Wow!" How cool is that! "What else do you

know about the Talisman?" I asked Lord Avalon.

He looked me straight in the eye and whispered, as if what he was telling me was a big secret. "The Talisman of Truth will open any lock, speak any language and show you the truth behind any lie. It can lead you on journeys to other lands and much more – I suspect you are only just discovering the real power of the Talisman, but you must always keep it safe."

Show me the truth behind lies? Take me to other lands? What did that mean?

"How do I get it to do those things?" I asked.

"The Talisman will work for you when you need it most," Lord Avalon smiled. "I am pleased, Will, that I met you. Now I know the Talisman is in good hands. Now I know that it is safe."

"Why do you care so much about the Talisman?" I asked. "Why do you care so much about me?"

"I had a visit from a man and woman when I was a young boy," Lord Avalon said, his eyes glazing over as he remembered. "They had lost their son and were travelling through time trying to find him."

People travelling through time, trying to find their son – I knew instantly that Lord Avalon was talking about my mum and dad.

"Your parents knew they didn't have long before they were separated," Lord Avalon told me. "They told me to find you – to bring you to me and ensure that you had the Talisman."

"Why did Mum and Dad come to you, and not me?" I wondered. "And why do they care so much that I have the Talisman?"

"Let me ask you, Will," he said. "What do you want most in the world?"

"My parents back," I said without thinking. There was nothing I wanted more.

"Well, the Talisman of Truth can lead you to them, all you need to do is ask."

"How?" I asked quickly.

"Let the Talisman lead you to where you need to go. Don't question where it takes you – just follow."

He smiled at me, "Let me help you get started." I think he could see by the look on my face that I had no idea where to begin. "When you are back in your own time, come back to this room."

"But there's no…"

"Lock?" he smiled. "The Talisman of Truth can open any door."

There was a knock on the door and Barnaby came in with Zoe.

"I think it's time we went home," Zoe whispered. "Egbert's happy here, and the knights can rest now they know you have the Talisman."

"Let's just slip away," I suggested to Zoe.

"Good idea," she said. "Don't want to risk Egbert crying and setting fire to everything!"

The knights were busy congratulating Egbert, but Lord Avalon turned around and smiled at me. I waved at him and he nodded and waved back.

Before he had a chance to say anything, I fired up the time machine and Zoe and I climbed in.

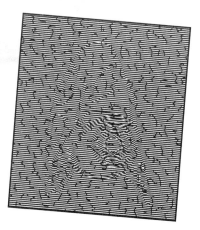

CHAPTER TEN
LORD AVALON'S STUDY

"Do you have ANY idea how worried everyone was!" bellowed Mrs Jones so loudly my face rippled. "You silly girl! And why are you wearing those ridiculous clothes?"

"I'm sorry," said Zoe feebly. Mrs Jones was FURIOUS about Zoe running away (well, that's the story Zoe gave her – she didn't tell her the truth about where she'd really been – obviously).

"Detention for you as soon as we're back at school, young lady!" Mrs Jones looked us both up and down. "Now go upstairs, get dressed and run to Mr Mills's history class as quickly as you can!"

Zoe and I headed upstairs towards the

dormitories. Mrs Jones glared at us until we were out of sight. It felt weird being back in the castle – it felt more like a museum now. It was nothing like the smelly castle it once was.

"The last thing I want to do is sit through a history lesson," Zoe groaned. "I want to go to bed," she yawned. "I'm exhausted."

"We probably know more about the castle's history than Mr Mills!" I joked. "We should be teaching the history lesson, not him!"

Zoe laughed as we both went our separate ways into the dormitories.

The boys' dormitory was empty when I went in. My bed was the same crumpled mess I'd left it in the night before. I'd been in medieval times for days, but the time machine had brought us back just a few hours after I left – just enough time for Mrs Jones to notice I'd gone. Great –

Morph was always getting me in trouble!

Something was sitting on my pillow. A letter!

WHERE DOES A GHOST GO TO PARTY?
ANYWHERE HE CAN BOO-GIE!

YOU'RE VERY NEAR TO FINDING YOUR PARENTS,
WILL. DO AS LORD AVALON SAID. VISIT THE ROOM
AT THE TOP OF THE STAIRS. LOOK BEHIND IT.

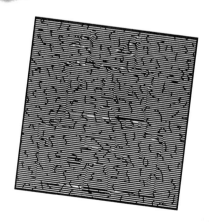

Look behind what? I wondered.

I was still wearing my pyjamas when I ran outside the dormitory to meet Zoe.

"Will, why haven't you got dressed?" she asked, annoyed. "Don't you think Mrs Jones is mad enough?"

"I need you to cover for me," I begged. "I've had another letter – there's something I need to do before we leave."

"What?" she asked.

"Will, Zoe!" screamed Mrs Jones from out of sight. "Downstairs now!"

"Please, Zoe," I said. "I wouldn't ask if it wasn't important."

"Fine!" she rolled her eyes and walked towards Mrs Jones's voice. "Will's already gone to class," I heard her say.

I took the opportunity to run as fast as I could

towards the staircase that led to Lord Avalon's study.

The staircase was just how I remembered it the night I first discovered it – dark and well trodden. The picture of Lord Avalon hung on the wall next to the door with no handle or lock.

I felt the amulet around my neck – the Talisman of Truth – begin to get warm as I approached the door. I pulled the Talisman out from beneath my T-shirt and watched as it glowed brighter than the sun. There was a loud click, as if a key had been turned in a lock. When my eyes got used to the brightness of the amulet, I noticed that the door to Lord Avalon's room had opened.

Quietly, I pushed the door open further and walked in.

The room looked just like it had in medieval times. There were piles of books on wooden tables, it smelt of spices and the air was heavy with dust. A thick layer of cobwebs coated everything in the room.

My heart nearly burst in my chest as I noticed what was on the far wall of the study.

Above Lord Avalon's throne was a painting. A painting that I hadn't seen before. It was the only thing in the room that seemed to be different from when I was in there talking to Lord Avalon.

I knew instantly that it was the picture the letter had told me to look behind.

The painting was of my mum.

Only she didn't look exactly like Mum – she wasn't wearing her usual clothes or her normal hairstyle. She was dressed in old-fashioned clothes and had flowers in her hair. I found myself walking towards the picture with my mouth wide open.

There was no mistaking the truth – it was definitely my mum in the picture.

There was a name plate by the picture, but it didn't say 'Eddy Solvit'. It said 'The Seismic Siren'.

I stood on Lord Avalon's throne and gently lifted the painting off the wall. I laid it down on top of a pile of books that were stacked on Lord Avalon's desk.

There was an envelope with my name on it taped behind the picture. I ripped the letter open, and this is what it said:

WHY DOES IT TAKE PIRATES SO LONG TO LEARN
THE ALPHABET?
BECAUSE THEY SPEND SO LONG AT C!

YOUR MOTHER HAS BEEN TRAPPED IN TIME, WILL.
SHE'S BEING HELD PRISONER AND IT IS TIME FOR
YOU TO RESCUE HER. YOU WILL FIND HER:
- AFTER A JOURNEY AT SEA
- IN THE PAST
- IN THE SEISMIC SQUARE

At last I had clues that would lead me to Mum!
Finally, I could set out on my greatest Adventure
yet. After all this time, I was going to find my
mum and bring her home.

CHAPTER ELEVEN
MORE CLUES IN
THE DIARY

I'm an Adventurer who time travels, solves mysteries and saves the world – my life will never be normal. But life has felt even less normal since I found out that Mum was stuck in the past – in the Seismic Square, whatever that is.

All I could think about was getting my next Adventure under way and bringing Mum home.

"You have to wait, Will," Zoe said, as we sat down on the school coach ready for the loooong drive home. "There's no point going on an Adventure unless you have the right tools and food supplies, and you need to get some sleep. You don't even know where you need to go!"

"The date on the picture said 1804," I said, as the coach pulled away from Avalon Castle.

"Fine, but you don't know anything about the 'Seismic Square'…" Zoe stopped talking and pulled out her SurfM8 from her pocket. She started typing something on the keyboard at super speed.

"What are you doing?" I asked.

"Check this out!" she said, turning the screen of her SurfM8 towards me.

The Seismic Square

A square of ocean greatly feared by pirates. Legend has it that any boat that sails in to the Seismic Square is never seen again. The square is located off the east coast of America.

Wow!

That certainly gave me a lot to think about...
pirates...boats that are never seen again...

I was so tired that I fell asleep on the coach
and slept for the entire journey home. ZZZZZ

I was woken up by Mrs Jones shouting in my
ear, "Will! Wake up, we're back at school and
there's someone here to pick you up."

Rubbing the sleep from my eyes, I pulled
myself up from my seat and off the coach. Zoe
was waiting for me outside. "My mum's here,"
she said. "Call me tomorrow. We need to talk
about the Seismic Square and how you're going
to get there!"

"Sure," I agreed.

"Oh, and Will," Zoe whispered, coming close
to me, "well done on your knight Adventure –
you were ace!"

Zoe ran off and got into her mum's car, waving at me as it drove away.

Stanley was waiting for me in his car. Stanley is Grandpa Monty's driver. He's pretty cool and has helped me out with my Adventures before.

"Hey, Stanley." I slammed the car door as I climbed in and belted up.

Stanley drove off without a word – he hardly ever talks.

We soon pulled up outside Solvit Hall.

I heard Plato yapping excitedly as I got out of the car. Plato is Grandpa Monty's dog – he's super

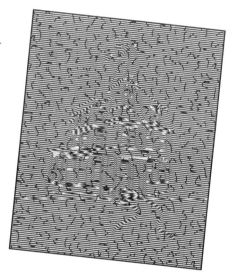

crazy!

"Hey, mate!" I smiled, as I bent down and wrestled Plato.

He yapped happily and licked my hand.

"Hungry, Mike?" Grandpa said from the  doorway of Solvit Hall. Grandpa never, ever remembers my name. I'm used to it now.

"I'm always hungry!" I replied, walking towards him.

"Good, good!" He hobbled back into the house on his walking stick. "The beef and chocolate stew is nearly ready."

Grandpa cooks the weirdest food. But I was so hungry, even beef and chocolate stew sounded tasty!

"Call me when it's ready!" I shouted, running up the stairs of Solvit Hall towards my bedroom with Plato following behind me.

Plato hopped on my bed as I slung my bag on my bedroom floor. I plonked myself down on the bed next to Plato and started stroking his fluffy white fur. He licked my hand in appreciation.

"I think my search is coming to an end," I whispered to Plato, who just carried on licking my hand. "I think I've nearly found Mum and Dad."

I bent down and pulled out the diary of clues that I'd started writing to help me find Mum and Dad.

starving!

THE DIARY
AND
CLUE RECORD
OF
WILL SOLVIT,
ADVENTURER

I opened the first page and added a few more clues to the list.

1. I will find one parent before I find the other.
2. Neither of them is where I left them.
3. The Partek said that my dad is in a place where I will never find him, but as they are human-hating cat-shaped aliens, I'm taking it with a pinch of salt.
4. Mum and Dad made a time machine that took them to the Stone Age.
5. Mum left Dad behind in the Stone Age and went off somewhere in the time machine.
6. Dad got into a Partek spaceship.
7. Mum is stuck somewhere between the Stone Age and the present.
8. Mum is stuck in the Seismic Square in the year 1804.

9. Mum is known as the Seismic Siren.
10. I will find Mum after a long journey at sea.

On the next page I added a few more questions I needed answers to.

- Why did Mum leave Dad in the Stone Age?
- Where did she go?
- Why did Dad get into a Partek spaceship when he knows they're the enemy?
- Where did he go?
- Where is he now?
- How will Mum and I get back from the Seismic Square?
- Will Mum remember me?

Then I turned onto a new page and wrote:

PLAN OF ACTION
- Time travel back to 1804.
- Find a boat that will take me to the Seismic Square.
- Find Mum in the Seismic Square.
- Bring Mum back to land.
- Time travel back to the present day.
- Find Dad.

As far as plans go, my plan of action wasn't great. There were loads of things that could go wrong. What if Morph took me back to the wrong time? What if I can't find a way out of the Seismic Square? What if I never find Dad again?

But my plan of action was all I had, and nothing was going to get in the way of finding Mum – not now that I knew where she was.

"Stew is ready!" Grandpa called from

downstairs.

Plato yapped and jumped off my bed and ran out the door.

I put my pen down and closed my diary. I couldn't wait to get my next Adventure under way – I couldn't wait to have Mum home again.

But first things first –

I was starving!

OTHER BOOKS
IN THE SERIES